WHY DO I SNEEZE?

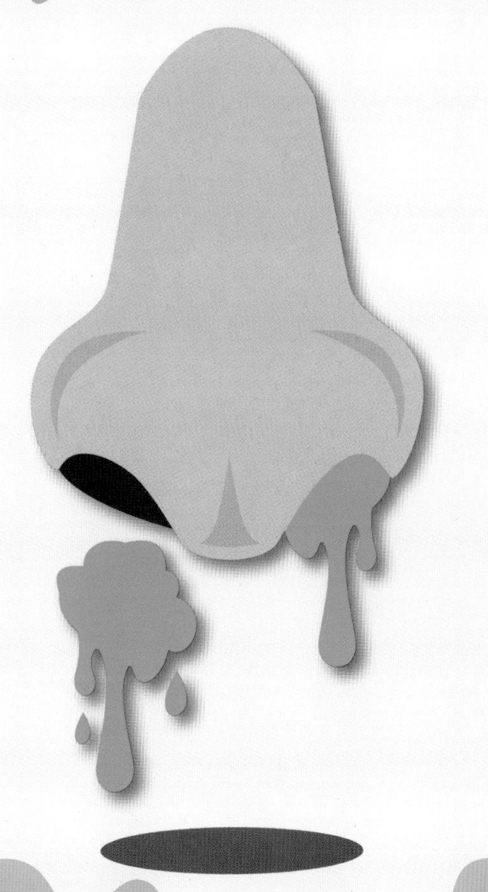

By Madeline Tyler

Published in Canada
Crabtree Publishing
616 Welland Avenue
St. Catharines, ON
L2M 5V6

Published in the United States
Crabtree Publishing
PMB 59051
350 Fifth Ave, 59th Floor
New York, NY 10118

Published in 2019 by Crabtree Publishing Company

First Published by Book Life in 2018

Printed in the U.S.A./082018/CG20180601

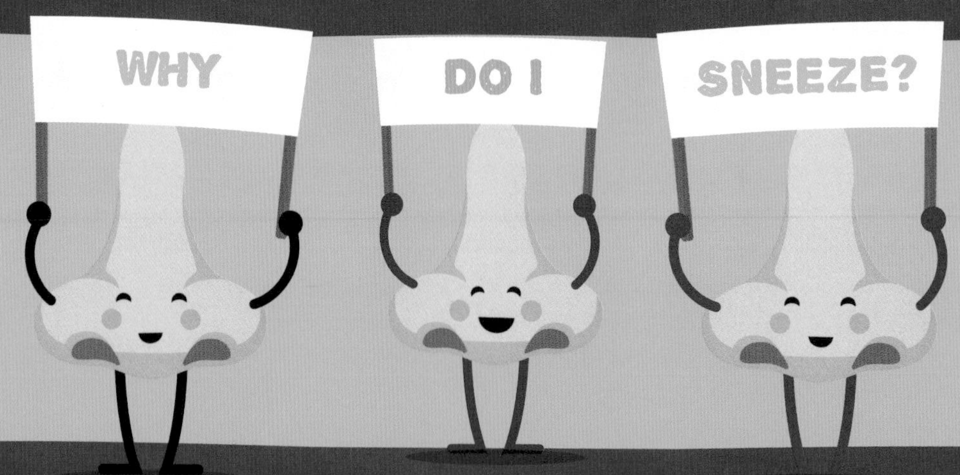

Author: Madeline Tyler

Editors: Holly Duhig, Kathy Middleton

Design: Danielle Rippengill

Proofreader: Janine Deschenes

Prepress technician: Samara Parent

Print coordinator: Katharine Berti

All facts, statistics, web addresses and URLs in this book were verified as valid and accurate at time of writing. No responsibility for any changes to external websites or references can be accepted by either the author or publisher.

Photographs

All images are courtesy of Shutterstock.com, unless otherwise specified. With thanks to Getty Images, Thinkstock Photo and iStockphoto. Front Cover & 1 – LynxVector, LynxVector. Images used on every spread – Nadzin, TheFarAwayKingdom. 2 – zizi_mentos, anpannan. 4 – Niwat singsamarn. 5 – Luciano Cosmo. 6 – didiaCC. 7 – Vetreno, robuart, moj0j0. 8 – TheFarAwayKingdom, CLUSTERX. 9 – Teerapol24. 10-11 – arborelza. 12 – Top Vector Studio, BlueRingMedia. 13 – yatate. 14 – robuart. 15 – naulicreative. 16 – Korbut Ivetta. 17 – Nadia Buravleva, Wor Sang Jun. 18 – Macrovector. 19 – toranosuke. 22 – Diego Schtutman, Nadezda Barkova, ershov Oleksandr. 23 – toyotoyo, Giraphics, Roman Marvel.

Library and Archives Canada Cataloguing in Publication

Tyler, Madeline, author
Why do I sneeze? / Madeline Tyler.

(Why do I?)
Includes index.
Issued in print and electronic formats.
ISBN 978-0-7787-5145-8 (hardcover).--
ISBN 978-0-7787-5151-9 (softcover).--
ISBN 978-1-4271-2175-2 (HTML)

1. Sneezing--Juvenile literature. 2. Human physiology--Juvenile literature.
I. Title.

QP123.8.T95 2018 j612.2 C2018-902409-7
C2018-902410-0

Library of Congress Cataloging-in-Publication Data

Names: Tyler, Madeline, author.
Title: Why do I sneeze? / Madeline Tyler.
Description: New York, New York : Crabtree Publishing Company, 2019. |
Series: Why do I? | Includes index.
Identifiers: LCCN 2018021334 (print) | LCCN 2018021667 (ebook) |
ISBN 9781427121752 (Electronic) |
ISBN 9780778751458 (hardcover) |
ISBN 9780778751519 (pbk.)
Subjects: LCSH: Sneezing--Juvenile literature. | Allergy--Juvenile literature. | Respiratory organs--Juvenile literature. | Human physiology--Juvenile literature.
Classification: LCC QP123.5 (ebook) | LCC QP123.5 .T95 2015 (print) |
DDC 612.2--dc23
LC record available at https://lccn.loc.gov/2018021334

CONTENTS

Words that look like **this** can be found in the glossary on page 24.

Got Snot?

Whether you are six or ninety-six, everyone gets snot. Everyone sneezes, too. But why?

A sticky slime inside your nose, called mucus, protects you when you breathe. Mucus catches anything harmful in the air before you breathe it in. You might know mucus better as snot!

Take a Deep Breath In

People breathe air to survive. Air **contains** a gas called oxygen, which our bodies need to survive. Air can be dirty and full of dust, **pollen**, and **germs** that could make us sick.

Dust and smoke make the air dirty.

Mucus is very important to your health.
It traps inside your nose anything that might harm your lungs.
Lungs are body parts that take in the air you breathe.

How You Breathe

Nose and Mouth

You breathe in air through your nose and mouth.

Mucus

Mucus is made by body parts in the mouth, nose, **windpipe**, and lungs. Mucus in the nose catches any dirt carried by the air you breathe.

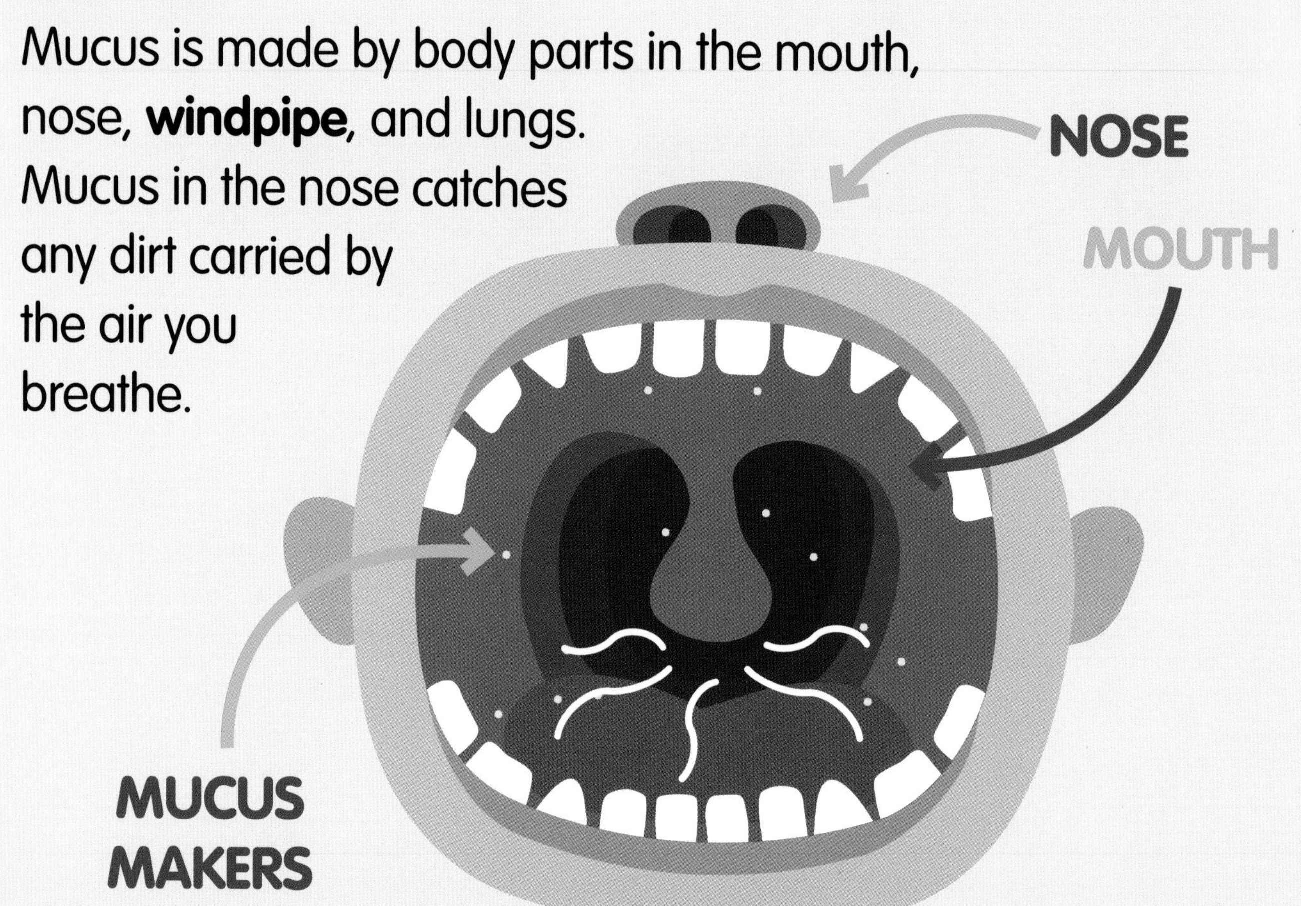

Windpipe

Air passes through a long tube, called the windpipe, into the lungs. Mucus and little hairs in the windpipe trap any leftover dirt.

Lungs

Your lungs breathe in fresh air and breathe out used air.

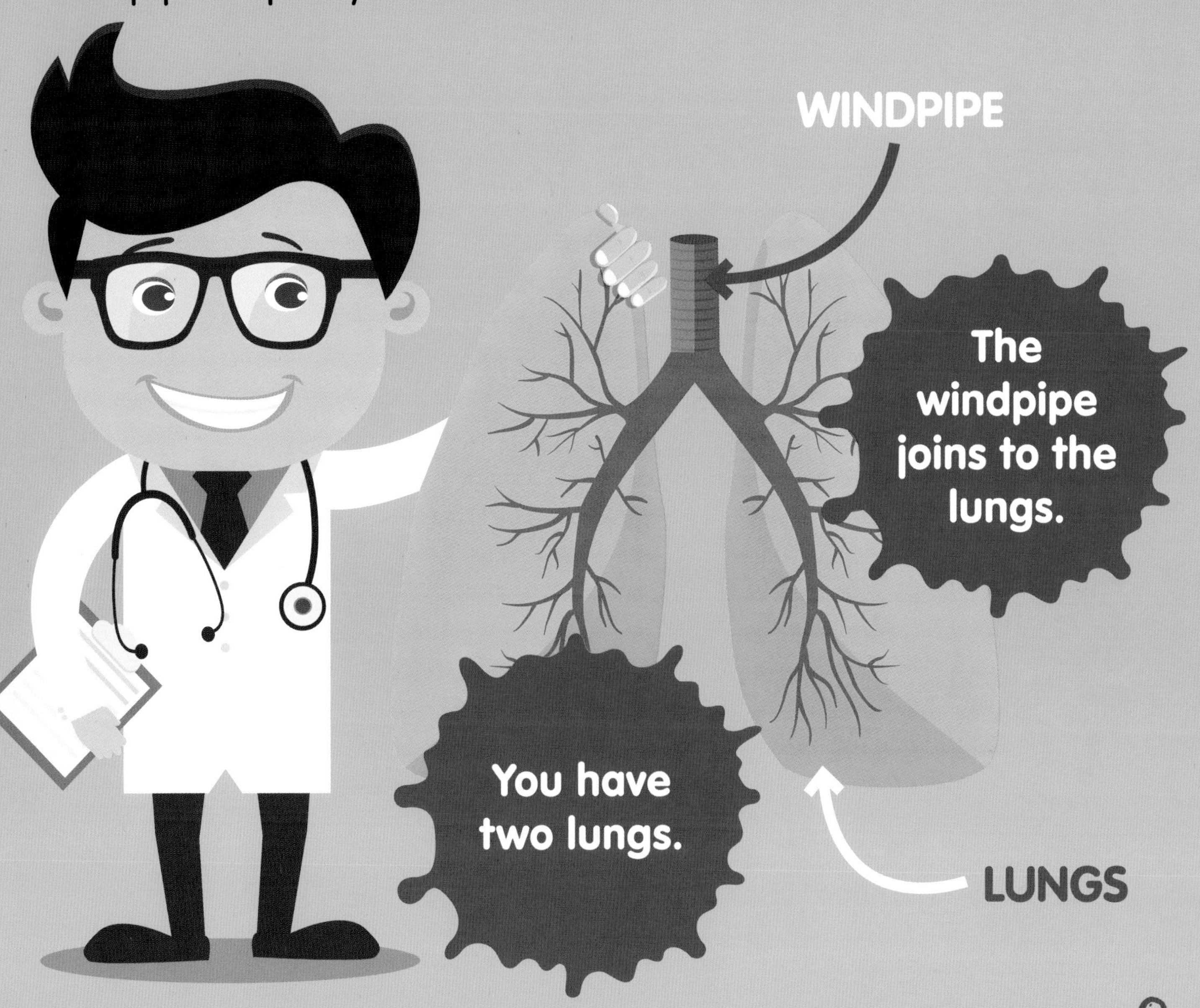

KEEPING OUT GUNK

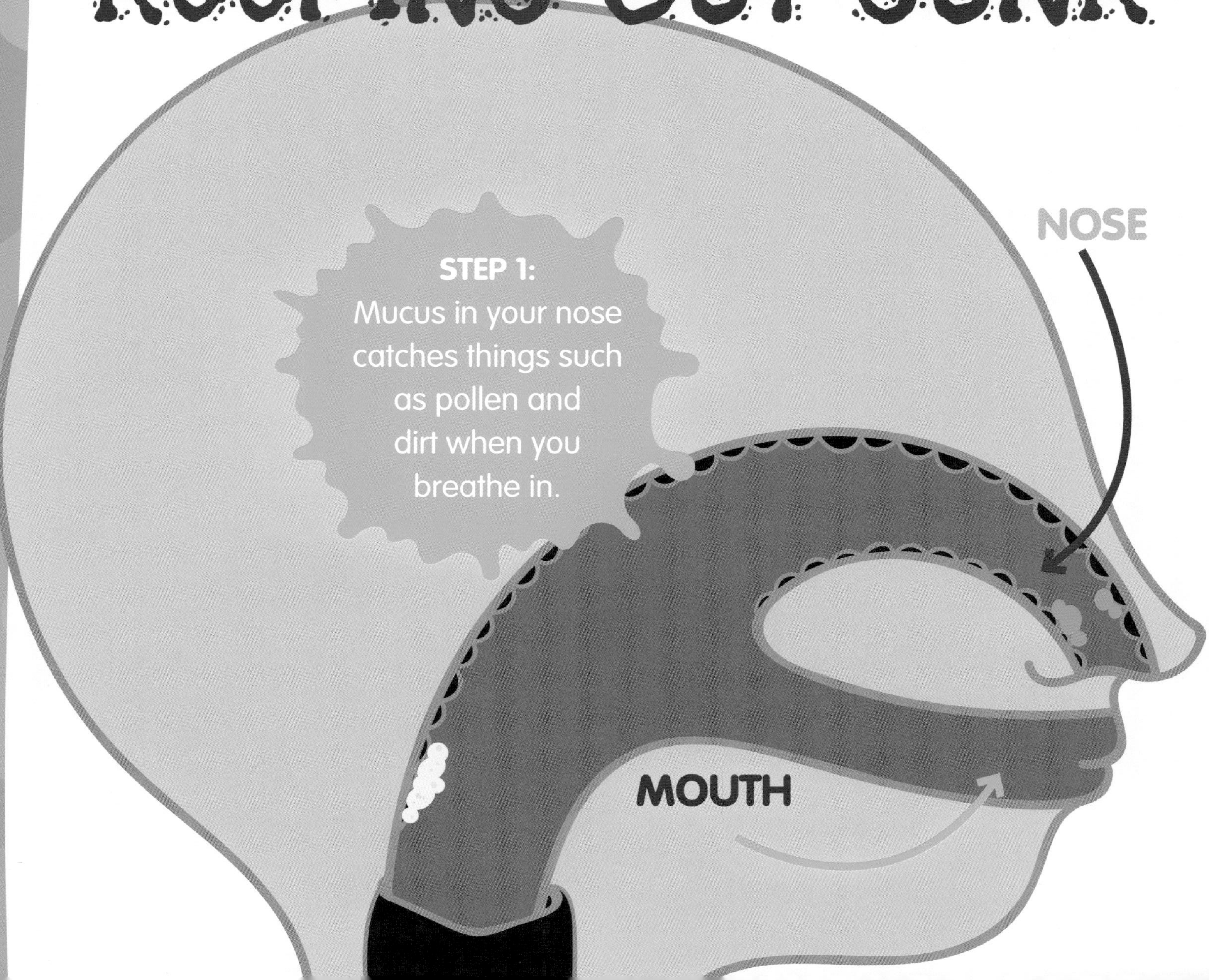

STEP 1:
Mucus in your nose catches things such as pollen and dirt when you breathe in.

NOSE

MOUTH

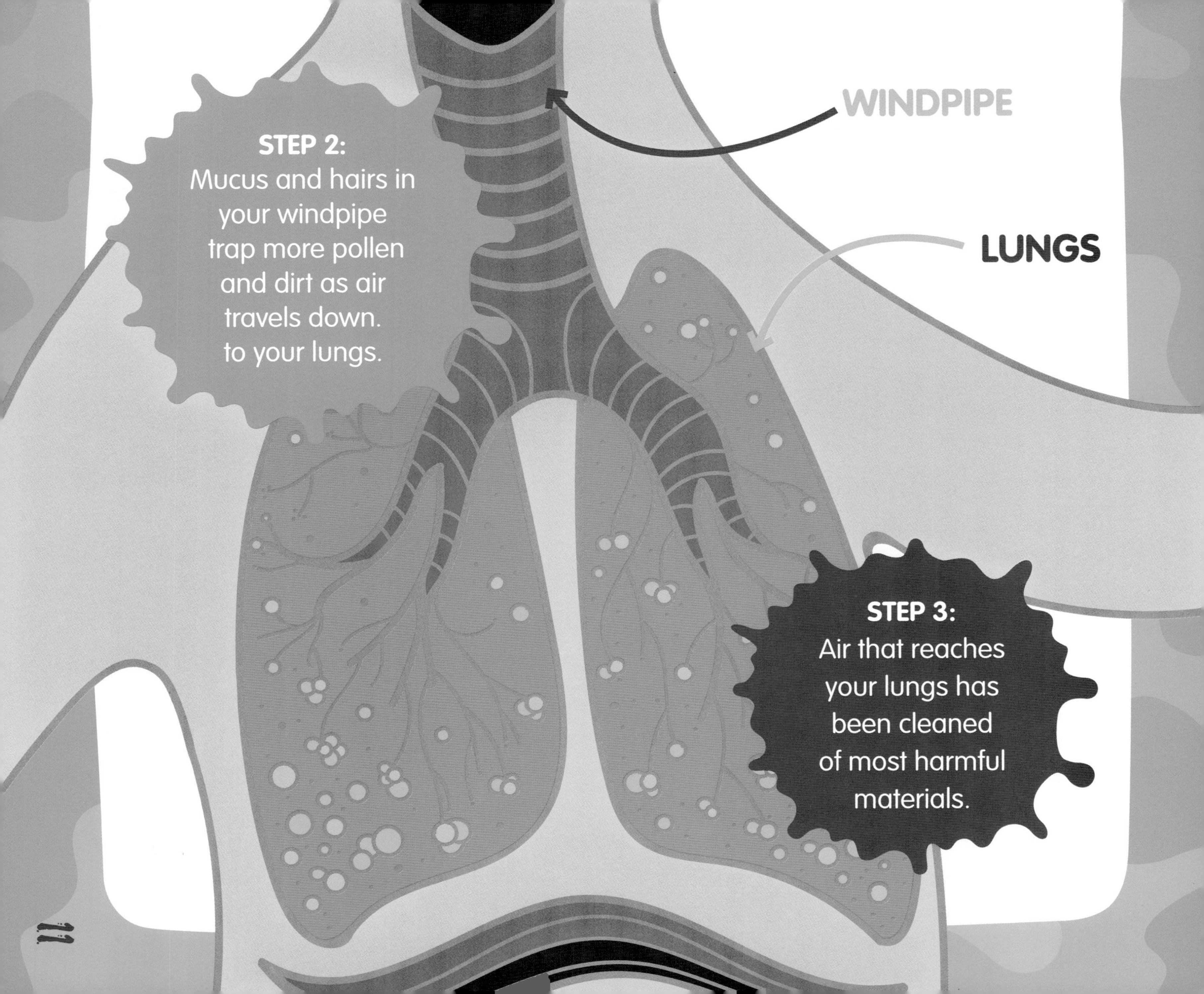

STEP 2:
Mucus and hairs in your windpipe trap more pollen and dirt as air travels down. to your lungs.

WINDPIPE

LUNGS

STEP 3:
Air that reaches your lungs has been cleaned of most harmful materials.

Blow your Nose

Most of the nasty things you breathe in get trapped in your snot. But, how does your body get rid of it?

Sometimes you swallow mucus, and a strong **acid** in your stomach destroys it. Other times mucus runs out of your nose or dries into hard pieces. Blowing your nose usually gets rid of this mucus.

Blow your nose into a tissue!

Invaders!

Some things in the air can make you sick. These are called germs. They often spread when people who are sick cough or sneeze.

Coughs and sneezes spread germs!

When you are sick, your mucus carries your germs. When you cough or sneeze, a small amount of mucus can spray the germs on other people and make them sick, too!

Mucus can turn green when your body is fighting an illness.

Coughs and Colds

Colds are **contagious**! That means you can catch a cold from someone else. Germs can be passed from person to person by a sneeze or on a person's hands.

It is very important to wash your hands to kill any germs when you have a cold. You should also cough or sneeze into a tissue to help stop the spread of germs.

Allergies

Some people have allergies to things such as pollen or animal fur. An allergy is a reaction to something which can make you feel itchy and sneezy.

Many people have allergies to cat fur!

Everybody breathes in pollen. But for people who are allergic to pollen, their nose will become irritated. Their body will make a lot of mucus to trap the pollen. They will also sneeze a lot to try to get rid of it.

What Snot Have You Got?

What does the color of your mucus mean?

Black means you have breathed in dirt, dust, or smoke.

A reddish color comes from a little bit of blood. The inside of your nose can bleed if it is dry. Tell a parent or caregiver if you see a lot of blood in your snot.

Yellow means you are starting to get over your cold.

Green means your body is fighting a cold.

Clear is the normal color of mucus.

Bogey Basics

Droplets from a sneeze can fly nearly 33 feet (10 m) through the air!

Insects and **amphibians** cannot sneeze!

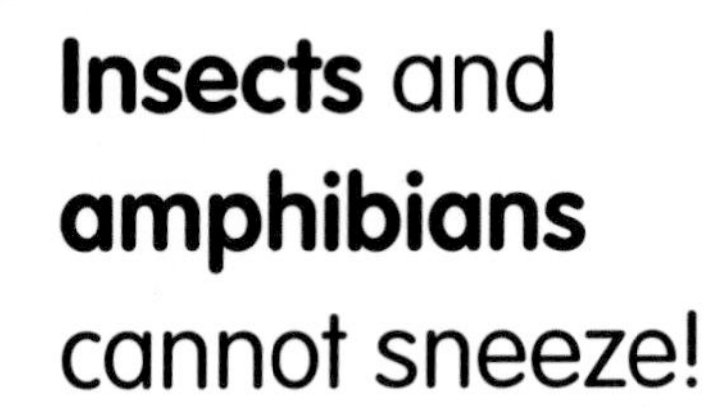

Your nose makes more than 1 quart (1 L) of mucus every day. It makes even more when you are sick!

You cannot keep your eyes open when you sneeze. Try it!

Sneezes can travel 30 to 60 miles per hour (45 to 95 km per hour)!

Donna Griffiths holds the Guinness World Record for the longest sneezing fit. She sneezed for 978 days in a row!

Glossary

acid A substance that can help break something down

amphibians A cold-blooded animal, such as a frog, that can live in and out of water

contagious Can be spread from one person to another

contains Has or holds something inside

germs Tiny living things that cause diease, or make us sick

insects Small animals with segmented, or separated, body parts and that often have six legs and wings

pollen The yellow dust found inside flowers

windpipe The part of the body through which air passes from the throat to the lungs